The Berenstain Bears ON THE JOB

A FIRST TIME READER™

The Berenstain Bears
ON THE
Stan & Jan Berenstain
Random House New York

 Published in the United States by Random House, Inc., New York, and simultaneously in Canada by Random House of Canada Limited, Toronto.

Library of Congress Cataloging-in-Publication Data: Berenstain, Stan. The Berenstain bears on the job. (A First time reader) SUMMARY: Two young bears speculate on all the things they could grow up to be, including a bus driver, farmer, scientist, singer, and computer programmer. [1. Occupations—Fiction. 2. Bears—Fiction. 3. Stories in rhyme] I. Berenstain, Jan. II. Title. III. Title: Berenstain bears. IV. Series: Berenstain, Stan. First time reader. PZ8.3.B4493Bhe 1987 [E] 87-9739 ISBN: 0-394-89131-7 (trade); 0-394-99131-1 (lib. bdg.)

Manufactured in the United States of America 21 22 23 24 25 26 27 28 29 30

In Bear Country, friends,
there are many kinds
of work to be done.
If you pick the right job,
work can be fun.

Let's take a Bear Country
tour and see
what you and we
can grow up to be.

HONEY ST

We could fight fires
like Firebear Bob.
Yes, that would be
an exciting job.

Or be a policebear
like Marguerite.
She tells us when
to cross the street.

If we don't obey,
she says—

We could learn to drive,
and drive a bus—
like Beartown driver
Grizzly Gus—

or an ambulance,
a truck, or a cement mixer!

BEAR COUNTRY
AMBULANCE
AMBULANC
TRUCK CO.

And don't forget
fixing things—

because almost everything
we use
sometimes has to have
a fixer!

You could be a teacher
and teach cubs how
to read and spell.

Be a doctor
and make folks well.

Have a store
and sell good things
like bread and honey!

Have a bank
where folks can
safely keep their money.

The engineer
tries to find
a better way
to do things.

The scientist
studies nature
to try to find out
new things.

You could be a builder
and build buildings
great and tall.

Be a wrecker
and wreck things
with your wrecking ball.

A singer!
To be a singer
is my choice!

That's fine.
But do you have
a singing voice?

On second thought,
I don't think I should.
My singing voice
is not so good!
That's all right.
Do not fret.
Our job tour is not
finished yet.

So many things
to be and do.
What you choose
is up to you.

All kinds of work
from which to choose:

an anchorbear—
and give the news,

an astronomer—
and count the stars,

an astronaut—
and visit Mars!

Be a programmer—
and work with computers,

an environmentalist—
and catch polluters!

A beekeeper—
and work with bees,

a forester—
and watch for fires
among the trees.

Be a carpenter—
and work with wood.

Say—could we have a farm?
Yes! Yes, we could!

We could raise
a champion pig.
And he will be
VERY big!

1ST
PRIZE

Farmers keep
the food bins full.

And, oh, yes—
a word of warning
to future farmers:

Always watch out
for the bull!

So many things
to be and do.
But if you haven't found
the thing for you...

No need to worry,
no need to fret.
The thing for you
may not have been
invented yet!

So remember, friends,
so many kinds
of work to be done—
just pick the right job
and work will be fun!